Misty is a stay-at-home mom of three kids and has been married for 2 years. She enjoys cooking and reading the latest crime novels. Horror movies and scary stories are her favorite things to curl up and watch and read. She lives in the Blue Ridge Mountains of VA and loves to chat with her fans.

To my husband, Michael, whom I wouldn't have done this
book without.
To my children, I love you more than words. You are my
reason for getting up every morning.

Misty Pegg

THE NIGHTMARE OF DRISCOLL

A Matt Cartwright Book

AUSTIN MACAULEY PUBLISHERS™

LONDON • CAMBRIDGE • NEW YORK • SHARJAH

Ordering Information
Quantity sales: special discounts are available on quantity purchases by corporations, associations, and others. For details, contact the publisher at the address below.

Publisher's Cataloging-in-Publication data
Pegg, Misty
The Nightmare of Driscoll

ISBN 9781641825849 (Paperback)
ISBN 9781641825856 (Hardback)
ISBN 9781647508401 (ePub e-book)

Library of Congress Control Number: 2024908840

www.austinmacauley.com/us

First Published 2024
Austin Macauley Publishers LLC
40 Wall Street, 33rd Floor, Suite 3302
New York, NY 10005
USA

mail-usa@austinmacauley.com
+1 (646) 5125767

To my Editor and Publisher, thank you for believing in me.

Chapter One

Officer Matt Cartwright was having a bad day. First, his car wouldn't start, then he had a flat tire on the way to work, which made him late, and then he found out he was getting a new partner because he had suddenly moved. He hated change. Why couldn't things stay the way they were? He didn't need a new partner after 10 years in the field; he knew what he was doing. Grumbling, he started his paperwork, which he might as well finish so he could close this case. Suddenly a shadow fell over his desk. He looked up before a smile broke out.

"Jim, well, I will be damned. How are you? What has you up this way?" Jim Holly was a 20-year-old veteran who was as good as they came.

"Hi, Matt, I guess I'm your new partner, a rookie." As he went to answer his phone rang, he picked it up and said, "Cartwright listened," then hung up. "Let's go, Jim got us a call."

Traffic accidents were the worst. Especially when the one who got hurt was the innocent one. As they finished up at the scene, they started talking about old cases. Jim was talking about some of the weirdest ones he had ever seen. "I once saw a guy stage a skeleton as a body so someone would come to his house. He was lonely."

Jennifer dropped her keys as she tried to open the door. She could hear the phone ringing. Please please don't hang up. She knew that the company was supposed to call today, but why did it have to be now?

Finally getting the door open, she dropped everything and picked up, "Hello hello hello, I'm here," only to hear a dial tone. She hit play on her machine while she picked up the bags and closed her door. You have six new messages she heard as she started putting things away. The first was a hang-up; the second she could hear someone breathing, then a hang-up. Two more messages were nothing. She heard the company call and walked over to hear, *We were trying to reach Jennifer Moore. This is Deborah, and we are sorry to inform you that the position has been filled. If you have any questions, please call us back.* She just sat she really needed that job and could have sworn she had gotten it. The last message started to play, and she jerked to attention. A man was talking; at first, she couldn't make out the words, then he got louder. *I love how you look when you undress at night. Those red panties you wore last night were hot; you just had to stop and look right at me, didn't you? I know you see me and you love me, but you seem to ignore all that I do for you. I want you to know that you are mine. Do you understand?* Panicking, she grabbed the phone and dialed 911 as she ran out of the apartment.

Matt and Jim were headed back to the office when they got the call and changed directions. As they arrived, they could hear a woman shouting, "What do you mean there is nothing you can do? This guy can obviously see me at night, and I'm scared." He walked up, and the first thought was, *What is going on?*

"Miss Moore I'm Officer Cartwright. Can you step over here to talk to me while my partner talks to the uniforms?" Huffing, she walked over.

"Are you going to help me?"

He said, "First tell me what happened?" As she started talking, he wondered how the guy saw her.

After talking to her, he said, "At this point there isn't much to go on. Is there somewhere you can stay for a while? Getaway maybe get a dog for protection, change your number, start over."

"Great," she said. "I get a creepy call and I have to uproot my life."

"We will be glad to increase patrol around here, but at this point we don't have many options."

"Great, thanks for your help," she replied sarcastically. "Is there anything else?"

She said, "Not right now."

"Here is my card. If you need anything, don't hesitate to call." Once in the patrol car, he wrote down notes while he waited on Jim.

"What do you think?" he said as Jim slid into the car?

"Maybe an ex-boyfriend playing a joke? I don't know she seemed scared. Let's put in for an officer to increase patrol around here and check back in a couple of days," he replied.

The next morning, he walked into work whistling; it was a beautiful day, and he was looking forward to his 4-day weekend coming up. Falling into routine, they started to put the case files they had on the computer. Looking up, he said to Jim, smiling.

"Going digital is supposed to be good, but it falls to us lackeys to do the work, which isn't so good. How about before the end of the day? We swing by and check on Miss Moore," he asked.

"Sounds good," Jim replied.

"I forgot about this case," he said holding up a file. "This is a girl who just disappeared; her name was Jane Mathews. Walking home from school, 16-year-old Jane was last seen with friends before they split to go home, and no one heard from her ever again. We looked for two years with no leads. Never any ransom or demands no body nothing just vanished."

Many grueling hours later, they packed up and headed to the car. Driving over, they spoke about Jim's wife.

"How's she doing?" Matt asked.

"OK, I guess she is in Tulsa with her parents for a while. Everything OK?"

"Yeah, she just…" Drifting off as they pulled up, Matt noticed the tape, the ME van, and the media behind the tape yelling. Ignoring them, he walked to the door and stopped. The smell was overwhelming. Laying in the middle of the living room was what was left of Jennifer Moore. Everyone looked grim; not much was being said. Walking over, he saw that most of her was missing. The skin had been torn off of her body; her bones were crushed in her face; you could see stab wounds on the bones; and above her body was painted Whore.

"You need to see the calling card," said an officer. Looking up, he said, "What?"

"He left you a calling card," the young woman said again, "there on the counter." Walking over to the counter, he looked at the card he handed the victim the day before. Underneath his name and number were what appeared to be blood was the words your move.

Slamming his hands in his pockets, he walked out of the house to get a breath of fresh air.

"Matt, hey Matt," he heard and looked up to see his Captain coming over.

"Hey Captain, can you believe this?"

"I heard about the card. This guy sounds crazy. We have a psychologist coming in. As of now, your weekend is put on hold. Why don't you head home and get some rest and start fresh in the morning? Nothing will help Miss Moore right now anyway. There was nothing you could have done."

Sitting at his desk the next morning, he started the case file on Jennifer Moore. Putting in what he knew, he switched screens so he could start running like a criminal through the system. Once he had put it in, a red flag alert started blinking, and he was picking up the phone a second later.

"Yeah, Captain, you should come see this. Am I seeing this right he is asked there is 158 like crimes across the US? We need to call the FBI office and hand this over. This is above our jurisdiction, and my pay grade," he said looking grim.

The next morning, he sat at the table, looking around at the new faces, and thought about how he hated inner agency cooperation. Yeah, they would do all the work, and the FBI would get all the credit.

Looking at the file, he wondered what kind of person got out of bed in the morning and thought, *Hey, I'll just go and skin a person. That took a special kind of twist.*

"Hello all I am special agent Christina Fields. The files you see in front of you are the 158 victims that have been killed and skinned. This guy is methodical and precise; he stalks them and terrifies them before killing them. All of them are skinned, some all the way, some half no skin is ever found at the scene, and they are all drained of their blood. We don't know what he does with the skin or blood at this time."

Putting up an image, she said, "This is Jane Doe 1; she is a mid-30s Caucasian female and was found on February 25, 2013 laying outside on a park bench with no clothes and the word WHORE painted on a sign hung by her body. ME has ruled it homicide; there is evidence of rape and mutilations over 300 stab wounds; flesh was ripped off her body; and her blood was drained. Her face is so mangled that we were not able to get identification."

"This is Jane Doe 2. She is a 58-year-old Caucasian female who was found on March 4th. Only this time, she was in a parking garage with no clothes, evidence of rape, mutilations, and over 300 stab wounds. Her flesh was ripped off her body, and her blood was also drained. No facial recognition available at this time. She too had the word WHORE painted above her body."

"This is John Doe 3. He is an African American male in his mid-30s who was found at a bus stop without clothes, the same as the other women. This is the most violent one that we have seen, with over 1000 stab wounds, skin ripped off, and his blood drained. These were his first three victims that we can pinpoint. After that, they become regular."

"The media has dubbed this guy 'Skin' because he skins his victims and poses them naked in public. Our psychologist thinks it has something to do with religion due to the way he poses them."

"As of now, we know he is here in Driscoll, TX, and we are going to work on catching this guy."

Officer Martinez stuck his head in the door. "Sorry to interrupt, Cartwright. You have a call picking up. He listened and hung up. That was dispatch. We have a second woman calling about being stalked." Christina spoke up, "Take agent James with you and see if this is our guy. I will get started on getting a stakeout set up."

On the way over, agent James was silent before he asked, "How many serial killers have you chased?"

"This is my first you, and it's the most hideous, yet I mean skinning my god some of those women."

"Let's focus on this woman and see if we can save her," Matt replied.

As he got out to knock, he noticed the barking of a dog, and the curtain moved. Looking around, he realized the road was black and empty. As they walked up the door open, there stood a woman. She was 5'9" and weighed roughly 158 pounds skinny thing he noted then he saw her eyes, they weren't terrified; they were angry.

"Officer Agent, please come in. I'm former FBI agent Sarah Jennings. I just moved here three months ago after I left the field."

"I'm Officer Cartwright, and this is FBI Agent James. Can you tell us what made you call us?"

"Yes, today I was reading and a call came in. I almost didn't pick it up because it was a blocked call, but after all the hang-up calls lately, I figured I would see who it was. This guy was talking low, like he was chanting. I could barely hear him until he said, 'I know you hear me. Sarah, I love how you look sleeping. You're so peaceful. What do you dream of? Do you dream of me and how I am going to take you? Or do you dream of all those other men you have? Sarah, you are mine; you will always be mine.' It took me a second to realize he had hung up before I picked up my cell and called 911."

"There will be an officer with you until we figure this out," Matt said. "I will take the first shift."

Chapter Two

Over the next several days, he spent all his time with her, talking to her and tracking where she went. Each city she stayed in, what she did, and how long she stayed. They ate and spent every minute together. She was a funny lady, and they laughed at so many things. He found out that they had a lot of movies in common, so he told her he would pick one up for that night and he would provide dinner. When she walked in, he said he hoped she liked spaghetti and that he had it delivered from his favorite restaurant. Walking to the cabinet, she picked out a bottle of wine and poured them each into a glass. They lingered over dinner, talking and laughing, and before he knew it, the bottle was gone and they had opened a second one. Taking their glasses to the living room, he popped in the movie and sat on the couch beside her.

As the movie played, Sarah sat beside Matt. She kept running her hand over his back and leaning into him. Looking up, he grabbed her and kissed her hard, then pulled away and said, "We don't want to do this. You're scared, and the wine is the one talking."

"Matt, it's OK," she said, reaching down and pulling him closer. Ripping her shirt, he started biting her neck and tits. Sucking one in his mouth, he rolled the other nipple between his fingers, pulling it taunt and pinching hard. Catching her breath, she moaned. Switching to the other nipple, he did the same to it. Reaching between her thighs, he pushed her skirt up and cupped her, pressing his hand into it. He could feel her heat through the skimpy fabric of her panties. Laying her down, he slid a condom on, then slammed into her. Making her scream, he put his hand over her mouth to muffle her. "Shhh, you don't want to worry the guards outside," he said, smiling. When he was sure she was done, he pulled out and rolled over to lay beside her. Are you OK "I didn't hurt you, did I?" he asked. Laughing, she replied, "That was perfect."

The next morning, Matt sat at his desk and went over all the files again. There must be something they were missing. Picking up one, he asked out loud, "What was the fiber that the ME had found?"

"I'm not sure it was just on this last one here in Driscoll," Christina said.

"So, all the victims were clean, but here. Does that make sense why the change? What makes this one different? I want to bring all these files to the table and open them up. Maybe there is a connection after all," he said.

"Matt, we went over this," Christina said. "We couldn't see any connection."

As they sat talking, Monica Banks couldn't believe she was stupid and hadn't noticed the gas gauge. She could have sworn she was on full duty this morning on the way to work, but here she was, stranded in the middle of nowhere. Picking up her phone, she noticed the bars were off. Figures no signal when she needed it. Hearing a car approach, she glanced up and saw a police cruiser pulling up. She hopped out as soon as he got out of the car.

"You OK?" he asked.

"No, somehow I ran out of gas."

"Don't worry, ma'am; we will take care of it. Do you happen to have a gas?" he asked.

"I don't think so," she said biting her lip and looking at her car.

"That's OK; we can buy one at the gas station. Why don't you lock up your car and we can go to the store?" Looking back, she thought she saw a shadow but wasn't sure. Shrugging off the feeling, she thought to herself that it was the cops who would be OK.

"You will have to sit in the back due to all my stuff," he said as he walked her to the car and opened the door. Once she slid in and he had closed the door, she noticed the handles were gone. Sliding into the car, he started it and hit his turn signal. Pulling out swiftly, he slid the window closed between them.

"Officer, excuse me," she said. "Officer, you are going the wrong way. The gas station is behind us." Turning up the music, he continued to drive as she started screaming and banging on the window and doors. Several miles later, he pulled into a garage and turned off the car. As he went to get out, he pushed a button, and she slumped into the seat. Opening the door cautiously in case she was faking it, he saw that she was out. As he picked her up to carry her inside, he started whistling. He loved this work, and he loved the audience's reaction more. He only wished he could see some of their faces when they discovered the bodies instead of hearing about it.

Back at the office, Matt and Jim were talking about the options of who would look like Sarah best when she walked up. "Well, boy, it looks like we are going to be working together."

"What no way you're a civilian," Matt said as he stood up. "Captain, please tell me this isn't true; she could get hurt." Former FBI agent Jennings knows how to take care of herself, and after much persuasion, she pointed out that we don't have anyone as tall as she is, and the unsub will know that it's not her, and we don't know how he will react.

Seated at the desk Matt, Sarah, Jim, and Christina were in a circle going over her phone logs for the past six months.

"Why did you retire," Christina asked? "You were a great agent."

"I know," Sarah said, "but after I dealt with the last kidnapping case and we found the baby dead, I just couldn't do it anymore."

"Tell me more about the case," Matt said.

"It was last March when we got a call from a retired Master Sargent of the Army. He had come home from shopping one day to find his wife dead and their eight-month-old baby gone. We were called in when the kidnappers requested a million dollars in ransom. Tracing calls and going over suspects got us nowhere. The calls would come back to the house, and he knew no one. They had just moved to Maine a month before so he could work as a security guard for a family friend. After a week of no contact, he woke up to find his baby dead on the porch. I couldn't do it anymore," she said. "So that day I handed in my resignation and took my last two weeks as leave. I bounced around some place to place, and about five months ago, the hang-up calls started. At first it was just hang-ups, then they started staying on longer and breathing, and finally some guy started talking really low. I never could understand what he was saying, though. I thought it was the dad who was angry with me, but I don't think he was this angry." Putting the man's name on a piece of paper, Jim got up and walked over to his computer.

"I'm going to run him. Keep going."

"I finally settled here three months ago, found a cute house that was cheap, and figured I would spend my days reading and cooking. Now I have some stalker. All the calls are on a burner phone; no registration and no way to track. Tell me about more cases you had," Matt said.

"It's not someone I worked with or a case I worked on; I helped those people, Matt. I tracked down lost children. Yes," he said, "and the ones you lost might be the ones doing this. We have to look at every angle, Sarah, and I know you don't want to. I know it's hard, but we have to do this to stop the guy."

"Matt, please listen. I spent weeks with these families, and I would have been able to tell if they were crazy. Losing a child can cause someone to go crazy." Standing up, Christina held up her hand.

"Sarah, I agree with Matt. Let's take a minute to calm down, and we will restart."

Chapter Three

As they stood arguing, Monica came awake.

"Where am I?" she said.

"Shh, don't worry, everything will become clear," he replied.

"Who are you? What do you want?"

"We are going to send a message to someone." He responded as he picked up a torch. "Lighting it." He starts telling her about all the people before her and how much fun it was. "This time we have a couple changes to make," he says. She starts screaming and struggling to get free as he comes closer. Laughing, he keeps teasing her, putting it close to her face, then pulling away. Hearing her scream is like music to his ears. Finally, he decides enough play time and leans in to touch her face with it. "I loved the sound of the skin frying and smelling it." The first touch had her passing out. "Tsk tsk," he says. "It's a shame, but it will go faster without you fighting me," he says, laughing. As he worked, he whistled, thinking about the cop's face when he got the package he was going to be sending.

The next morning, as Matt lay in bed, he dreaded getting up, but he could smell the coffee. As he walked into the kitchen, he felt a breeze, turned to look, and froze. He saw his door open, and in the doorway was a package. Grabbing his gun, he swept each room, and once he was sure it was clear, he picked up his phone and hit a button. "Yeah, captain, he was here, and he left me a package. Yeah, I'm sure it has blood on the side. I'll be out front," he said. Stepping outside, he waited for them but couldn't help fight the feeling to go see what was left. It seemed like forever before he saw the dust of the cars pulling up. He noticed Sarah riding with Christina.

"What a way to start the day," said getting out.

"Yeah, it's a joy to wake up to a strange package and see everyone before coffee," he replied. Walking toward the house, they got as close as they could while a robot was sent to inspect the package. Turning, the captain said, "It's clean." Stepping forward, he replied, "Let's get it opened up then." Picking up the package, he went inside and grabbed a knife.

"Hold on," said Sarah. "Let's get pictures and document it as we go." Sighing, he sat the package down and stood back as she took some stills. Finally, she said, "OK, open it up." As he slid open the top, he almost dropped it to the floor.

"Jesus! What the hell!" Sarah exclaimed. There laying in the box was a set of human eyes, and written underneath in what appeared to be blood were the words, 'I'm watching you!' And a tape underneath it.

"I think we need to get this back to headquarters and get a meeting set up," Sarah said.

Once everyone was seated, Christina walked in.

"Well, guys, this is new. Unsub sent us a video of his latest victim. Matt, are you sure you want to see this?"

"Yeah, I can handle it," he said. Cueing up the video, she started it and then froze it.

"This is Monica Banks; we made an identification with facial recognition." Resuming the video, he sat silently as he watched the guy torment her and squeezed his eyes shut when he picked up the scalpel. Mumbling something, Matt said, "Wait, pause it," he said. Pausing the video, Christina turned. "What's wrong?"

"What did he say? I didn't hear it," he said.

"This will only sting a little," she replied. Turning around, she took a deep breath and hit play once again. They could hear the woman screaming and crying as they sat helplessly, watching her eyes get cut out. When it was done, the guy picked up a card that said, "It's your fault, Officer Cartwright, just remember this."

When the video faded out, someone said, "Can you replay it, but this time from the very beginning?" As it came on again, they could see it was very blurry and slowly came into focus. Sitting in the chair was the same woman zip-tied to it.

"Pause the video," someone said. "That is what I thought. That is a hydrogen-casting torch system, and those are not cheap. Those go for about three grand easily. There can't be too many people in the area who own them, can they?"

"Good catch. Can you start looking around to see who bought one and when?"

"I can try, but these things are sold a lot." They resumed the video to see the man in a black mask, black robe, and black gloves standing near the woman. Taking a deep breath, Matt sat forward. Pausing the video, Christina stepped forward again.

"We can guess from this video that the unsub is 5'9" with the clothes; it's hard to guess, but we figured a range of 240–280 pounds. We can't see his hands, face, or anything. As you can see, he keeps the camera focused on the woman, and the card never moves. Matt, you don't have to stay for this."

"Yes, I do. This is my fault," he said, "so let's see what we might have missed the first time." Resuming the video, they watch as the guy burns skin, cuts, stabs, and freezes the woman.

"Stop," said Jim. "What is that in his hands?" he asked. "I don't know," said Christina, "but let's get some pictures and go ask a couple of local hardware stores." Suddenly, Matt jumped up so fast that his chair went flying backwards. He stomped out of the room and slammed the door.

"I'll go after him," says Jim. He catches up to Matt at his desk.

"Hey man, you know this isn't your fault. This is just some sick guy messing with your head. Let's focus on Monica Banks. And try to save what is left of her." All day, as they ran names and addresses, they kept striking out. "Who knew how many Monica Banks lived around here?" he said angrily as he hung up the phone.

Finally, after midnight, his captain looked in and sent him home. "There is nothing more we can do tonight," he said. That night he tossed and turned, and the next morning he felt extra old as he walked into work. Getting almost to his desk, he heard the door open, and his captain poked his head out of the door. Dispatch just called and said they found a car abandoned on Route 665. The doors are locked, and there is a plastic bag in the window. Plates come back to Monica Banks. Jim was out of the chair before he finished the name. Running toward the elevator, Matt yelled over his shoulder, "Send me the location on my phone." Slamming the car door shut, Jim peeled out as he picked it up.

"Maybe we can get a lead now that we have some evidence." It seemed to take them forever to get to the car, but as they pulled, they saw the State Police officer walking toward them.

Opening his door, he said, "Morning."

"You made good time," the officer replied. "Yeah, we got a video of this woman yesterday and have spent the past 20 some hours trying to find her. Have you opened up the car yet?"

"Not yet," he said. "I was told to wait for you." Opening the car, they noticed the cell phone on the front seat, like it was tossed there.

"Well, this doesn't look good. From what I can see, she was taken from this spot."

"Why do you say that," said the state trooper? "Well, we have the bag on the car, no keys, no purse, and the phone is dead and tossed like she dropped it. There is no sign of a struggle and no blood." Looking in each direction, he said, "There is so much open road, she could be anywhere."

"Not much of a chance of following any tracks," Jim said.

Back at the prescient, they sat at their desk, writing up the case file for the car, when Jim stopped and looked at

Matt. "Hey Matt, do you think we could track her last movements?"

"Maybe we could grab a clue as to what happened." Looking as the elevator dinged, they saw an officer bringing in the mechanic who had come and towed her car.

"I figured I would let you know the gas line had been cut. It was a slow leak but a clean cut."

"This guy knew what he was doing," Jim said.

"Thanks," Matt said as he started retyping.

"How did he get to her car?" Jim said?

"Huh." Matt looked up.

"How did he get to her car and cut the lines without anyone noticing him?"

"I don't know," Matt said, "but I have to go home and think."

Christina walked over and said, "We are having a press conference. My boss thinks it's time to shine a little light on this situation, and maybe the public will help." Standing up, he said, "I will see you in the morning." All night, Matt looked over his notes again and again and couldn't figure out the connection. He didn't know how anyone could blame him, as far as he knew he hadn't made anyone mad at him. Hell, he went out of his way to keep the peace just so he didn't have to have an argument.

Going to bed that night, Matt couldn't help but think about what was happening to the woman. Across town, Sarah sat in front of the computer with the mouse in hand, but she couldn't bring herself to hit send. While she deleted the message, she only wished she could say something. In the garage, Trisha had come awake and was hyperventilating. "Please help; I can't see," she said. "Hello, anyone there?"

She heard a sound, turned her head, and felt the pain blossom. Screaming, she felt something hitting her face over and over. She could hear and feel the bones crushing. Laughing, the guy swung the hammer again, and a piece of her cheek fell off and went flying.

"Whoops," he said. "I hope you don't need that. Nah, you can let me have it for our next message." Picking it up, he watched her body lay there, the blood pooling out. Sighing, he hoped she would last a long time; she was the best one ever.

The next morning, Matt walked into work, and Harvey stopped him.

"A package came for you today."

"From where?" Matt asked.

"Some girl walked it in said it was urgent that you get this as soon as you came in."

"What did she look like?" Matt asked as he picked up a set of gloves off Harvey's desk.

"I don't know, just some currier."

"Uniform name?"

"I didn't see a logo anywhere," he said.

"What's this about, Matt?"

"I don't know, Harvey, but I have a bad feeling."

"Did you send this through the machine?"

"Yeah, it's clean, just some papers and something else inside." Sliding his keys under the tape, he opened the package and heard Harvey gasp.

There was half of her face with a message, 'Cheek Mate!' Kicking the wall, "Son of a Bitch," he said. "This isn't a game. What the hell does he want?" Breathing, he examined the card and noticed a logo on it.

"Does this have anything to do with the news report last night?" asked Harvey. As he went to answer, something caught his eye on the paper.

"What is that?" he asked.

"What was the uniform standing nearby? That logo—what is it?"

"I don't know. Get this to the lab ASAP." Getting in the elevator, he was more determined than ever to figure this out. As he got off the elevator, he met Sarah and Christina and told them what he had gotten.

"Matt, our shrink got in touch with us, and she recommends removing you from the case."

"Why would you do that?" he said angrily.

"Matt, this is personal. Someone is out to get you, or at least to make it seem like you know who is doing this."

"I know that, and that is exactly why I will catch this sorry bastard, but right now I need to do this," he said.

"What are you going to do?" Sarah asked.

"I want to start from the beginning; let's write everything down."

"OK, but let's go to the conference room; it is bigger." Gathering case files, he sat at the table and started flipping open the files. Looking up, he noticed other people were there looking.

"What are we looking for?" someone asked.

"Anything what bills they paid, what they ate, what they had in their house everything is now important; he chooses them somehow." As he started writing things down, he lost track of time. Half way through the files, he looked them up and called Jim over.

"Take a look at this," he said, handing him his list. As Jim sat down and started going through the list, he said, "Well, what do you think?"

"Hey, Christina," Jim said, "can you come over here? Yeah, what's up?" she said.

"I think Matt found out how he picks them." Everyone in the room went silent.

"What did you find," Sarah asked.

"Hold on, let me show you," he said as he started writing the things he had on the board and kept looking through the files to make sure he had it right. "According to their bank records, every one of our victims had been to the DR within three weeks of their death. Some had a prescription filled from the doctor all at their local pharmacy. All of them are single, live alone, and have no pets."

"So, who has access to the medical files?" someone asked.

"Officer Lendoff, that could be any number of people: you have the person who checks you in, the nurse, the doctor, sometimes an assistant, then you have the person who checks you out and schedules your next appointment, and that is all before we get to the people in the medical coverage group or anyone who was there that saw them."

"Our list just got huge," someone said in the background. Taking a marker, Christina started writing out a list of people and ideas of who would have access.

"Find out which doctor each person went to and the name, then we can split the list up and see what we find out." Knocking on the door had every head looking up. As it opened, they saw a new girl; her name was on the tip of his tongue when she said, "I got a lead. I talked to several companies and had my dad, who is a plumber, do some checking, and he found that object was actually a CO2 and nitrogen pipe kit. According to everyone I talked to, those aren't something that you can pick up in your local store."

"OK, now we have somewhere to start. Jim, you and Marissa start looking at companies and see if we can get a copy of customers who bought one of those that live in the United States. I don't care if we have to get a warrant. Mark Sarah, how are you doing on the hospital records?"

"It's slow," Sarah said. "Everyone keeps quoting patient privacy laws to us. Captain, time to call our attorney. Let's hand the ball to them."

After several days of phone calls and background checks, Matt was in a bad mood. Who was this guy and why him? It had been tense waiting to find out, but everything was slow, especially since they had to go to the attorney to lay out what they had, then she had to go to the judge and get multiple warrants for records, then warrants for information and for each company. He felt like it would never end. He heard the elevator ding as he went to pick up the phone, but was swiveling around as he heard the footsteps get near his desk. Looking up, he stopped all movement as the officer walked toward him with a package, and he stood up.

"Captain, come here!" Jim yelled. Walking out, his captain took in the scene and reached over to grab a pair of gloves before he took the package. Laying it on the desk, they took more pictures, and the Captain picked up a letter opener. Sliding it gently over the tape, they stood as it slid silently. Picking up one flap, he laid it back, and everyone strained to peek. Inside they found an ear with a note underneath that said, "I heard you were looking for me; maybe this will help." There was an address at the bottom.

"What the hell is this guy, 12? I mean, that's sick. Jim looked up from the computer."

"Matt, it's your mom's house."

Everyone jumped to their feet and headed out.

"Who knows where you grew up, Matt?" Jim asked.

"I don't know he responded. I grew up not far from here and didn't go far from home. My mom is old and sick; if this sicko does anything to her, I will kill him."

"Don't go there yet; let's go see your mom and make sure she is OK."

Pulling up, he didn't let Jim put the car into park before he was out of the door.

"Mom, are you home?"

Looking up, she said, "Matt, how nice. I was going to call you today."

"Mom, are you OK?"

"He saw that she was fine. Just yesterday, that nice doctor that you know was by to check on my health and to check on you. What doctor?"

"He left his card right here. Dr. Yearly, he said he was a friend of yours and wanted to see how you were handling your stress." Sitting beside her, he looked her over and was finally able to breathe as she saw that she was fine.

"Did he say anything else? Mrs. Cartwright asked Christina?"

"Oh, Matt, you didn't tell me that you had friends. Why don't I put on some tea for us and we can talk?"

"Mom, it's important to try and remember if this guy said anything else."

"Why? He only said that he would be seeing you soon, and he hopes you enjoy your gifts."

"Do you think you can describe him?" asked Jim. "Sonny, I can't tell you what you look like in 20 minutes, but I can remember what we talk about."

Sitting at the station Matt went over and over the boxes. Plain cardboard nothing on them. *"How do we track him?"* he asked out loud to himself. Looking up, he saw that everyone else had gone home, and it was a new shift. Closing down his computer, he almost called Sarah, but figured it was so late; she was probably asleep and he would talk to her in the morning.

He stood at the side of her bed, looking at her while she slept. She was so peaceful laying there that he almost had second thoughts that she was the one for him. As he stood watching her, he wondered what dreams she had. Soon she would dream of him, but not yet. He had other work to do. Walking back to the living room, he started working on the cop that interrupted him. Jerking awake, Sarah looked around, wondering what had woken her. She thought that she heard a noise, but she didn't know what it was. Looking around for Max, she remembered that he was at her friend's house since she had the cops around her. She noticed the door was open and could have sworn she had closed it when she went to bed. Getting up, she pulled on a robe. As she started walking out to the living room, she thought she smelled tobacco and started talking.

"Officer Green, you really should step outside." She started screaming, and in a pool of his own blood was the officer. Picking up her phone she pressed 1 and starts yelling, "Matt, he was here. Oh my god, Officer Green is hurt, possibly dead. Hurry Matt."

Jumping out of bed Matt grabs his gun and starts out of the house, realizing he is barefooted.

"What happened? Is he OK?"

"I don't know," she said leaning over him. "He has a faint heartbeat," and Sarah stated before hanging up to call 911 to get the ambulance there. Slamming his feet into boots, he jumps in his car and is at Sarah's house in record time. He flies out of his car, looking around at all the activity.

Matt it's bad, Christina met him at the door holding up her hand.

He knocked Officer Green out and started peeling his skin back. The EMT's found stab wounds and burn marks on him.

"He did all this to him in her living room while she slept?" he asked.

"He left another package, which she didn't see, thank God. We have her at a hotel with a doctor, but this is a new pattern, Matt."

"What was in the package?" he asked as he looked around.

"Her hand and the note underneath said so close yet not close enough. Guess you will need a hand from me to find me!"

"Is that woman still alive," he asked out loud. "Hopefully not. This is a sick, demented man."

Stepping fully into the living room, he could see the walls that were once a neutral brown, covered in blood.

"Matt, I want you to head to the hotel; as of now, you are Sarah's bodyguard. Where she goes, you go; what she does, you do. This guy has an infatuation with you, and we need you to start thinking about anyone who has a grudge against you or wants you dead," said his Captain.

Chapter Four

At the hotel, Sarah couldn't calm down. Maybe she should have let the doctor give her something to help her sleep. Picking up the phone, she called downstairs and asked the front desk if the doctor had come down and left yet. Telling her no, she asked them to send the doctor back up when they saw him in the lobby. When she heard a knock at the door, she didn't hesitate to open it and was hit in the face and knocked out.

Slowly coming awake, she struggled to look around, but her hair was in her face. As she tried to raise her hand, she realized they were tied up, and the sheet was pulled off her body.

When she saw the man in the corner, she started to struggle and scream. Getting up, he walked over to her as he pulled out a knife and said, "If you don't stop that, I will kill you, but only after I kill your dog in front of you. The last thing you will see is his bloody bones, and I can promise you it will hurt. You have seen my work."

She closed her eyes. She wouldn't give him the satisfaction of seeing her fear. He started laughing. "Well If I had known you were a fighter, I would have gotten you earlier."

"You thought you were smart going to a hotel, but I always get what I want," he says.

He leans down, leering at her. She notices the faint smell of tobacco on his breath mixed with something else. Something she can't remember, but it's familiar to her.

The next thing she feels is a searing pain in her cheek, which has her passing out. "What a shame," he says. "Time to get to work, don't you think, honey?" Getting the bag from the corner, he takes out his scalpel, torch, and whistles while he starts working on her. Keeping an eye on the camera he put in the bushes outside the hotel, he started working on her body.

Pulling up, Matt opened the hotel lobby door and walked in as he saw a man get off the elevator dressed in doctor scrubs. He said evening and moved over. The man seems to be in a hurry. Hitting the 12th floor, he waited patiently for the doors to open. When he got to room 1208, he realized something was wrong; the door was open a little. Pulling out his gun, he opened the door slowly and dropped it. "Oh my God, Sarah, it's OK." He pulled out his cell phone and dialed 911. "Officer down," he yelled, "get me EMT's immediately."

"It's OK, Sarah, hang on," he said as he waited. Pushing him to the side, the medic said, "Move so we can get her transported." Shortly after he sat in the waiting room, waiting for her to come out of surgery, he saw Christina and his Captain walked in.

"How is she?"

"I don't know they have her in surgery," he said as he saw a nurse step in. Looking around, she walked over.

"Are you here for Miss Jennings?"

"Yes, we are her coworkers," said Christina, pulling out her badge.

"How is she?"

"She is stable for now, but they are keeping her in a coma due to the injuries. We are transferring her to a room, and then you will be able to sit with her. We have to post a guard with her," said Christina.

"I will get with the hospital to set it up," replied the Captain.

"Tell me what happened," Christina said, turning to Matt. After going over everything, she asked if he could describe the doctor.

"No, he had a hat on and was almost running. I thought he had a call."

"Do you want to stay here or go to the office? We are having a meeting with all hands-on deck now."

"I'm going to stay with her for a while until we get the rotation schedule set up for her guard."

Back at the prescient, the meeting room was buzzing with people talking; no one could believe what had happened.

"Alright, people, settle down and find your seats. We have a lot to go over and not much time to do it," Christina said as she walked into the room. Waiting for everyone to quieten down, she put Sarah's picture up on the screen. "Some of you know her, and some have worked with her," she said as she started. "Tonight, our unsub slipped up and didn't kill his victim. This is Sarah Jennings, she is a 27-year-old Caucasian female single who lives at home with her dog and is an ex-FBI agent. Officer Matt Cartwright found her door open upon arrival at the hotel where she was put for protection. Miss Jennings was on the bed, covered in blood, unconscious. Her hand had been cut off, her face half of it ripped off. The skin on her leg, belly, and thigh all missing. She is currently at the hospital in a medical-induced coma until the doctors think it's safe to bring her out. As of now, leave is suspended. If you're working on a case, see me when it's closed. Let's get this man before he gets another one."

Sherrie was giving up on men; this was the last straw. She couldn't believe that jerk was trying to force her to have sex and then telling her to get out of the car in the middle of nowhere. The last time she met anyone online, she goes out. As she started walking, she leaned down and took off her shoes. It was going to be a long night. Looking back, she saw headlights and stepped to the side. *Please stop, please be nice, and please take me home*, she whispered to herself. Leaning down to the car, she said, "Can you help? I was left out here."

Smiling, the guy hit the unlock button. "Sure, where do you live?"

"About 8 miles into town," she replied.

"Sure, I can take you; just hop in." Sliding in the seat, she jerked back up and said, "Ouch something is poking me."

"I'm sure it's nothing," he responded as she slumped down. Pulling out, he turned the radio on while he laughed. He couldn't believe his luck.

The next morning, Matt's phone rang, and yeah, he answered. "We found Monica banks this morning," Jim said. "She was dumped outside of a house on 5th Street. Captain said to let you know, but he wants you to stay at the hospital. Sarah is your priority. How's the list coming?" Slow, he responded, "I'm supposed to go back 32 years for grudges. If anyone can do it, you can," Jim said.

"Time to wake up Sherrie." Slapping her face, he couldn't get her awake. Dan was getting angry. "Sherrie, come on, Sherrie, time to wake up." Feeling for a pulse, he found she was dead. "How dare you? he screamed as he picked up the hammer." You stupid bitch, "he screamed as he slung it into her body over and over, crushing every bone in her body. Breathing, he dropped the hammer. This was a mistake; he could fix it. Maybe the doze had been too high. Picking up the scalpel, he started working on the face. 'Bitch'. He carved in her face. Putting her in the car, he drove to the corner where the police station was and slowed down so he could reach over and roll her out. Picking up speed, he went around the corner. He drove off, wishing he could be around to watch when they found her, but he had a date to keep."

Pulling up outside the house, he saw the lights were still on. Taking a deep breath to calm himself down, he settled in to wait. This is what he was supposed to be doing. Stay on the path, and he will find his true love. She was his true mate, and tonight she would beg for him and finally understand she was his, just like she did all those nights of her teasing him. Twenty minutes later, he saw the house go dark. He pulled up his cell phone and saw her in her room. Looking right at him as she took her shirt off. He sat forward; this was the part he loved all the foreplay as she seduced him with her body. She paused and walked over, picking up her phone. He could see her laughing and talking. Who was calling her and interrupting their special time? How dare she stop and spend time with someone else? She was his, didn't she know that? Getting out of the car, he grabbed his bag to get to work. Walking up, he hit a button that turned off her power and blocked cell phone calls. He tried to open the front door and found it locked. As he walked around the back, he heard a dog barking and froze. Who's there he heard? Not moving, he saw the fence move. Turning, he ran, getting in his car. He slammed the door and sped off. How was it possible that she was supposed to be alone? What the hell was that?

As Jim sat at his desk, he looked for Matt but didn't see him. "Hey, Jim," said Christina, "want to take a drive?"

"Um, sure, where to?"

"We got a call. A woman reported an attempted break-in. The funny thing is that her power and cell phone went out a minute before it happened."

"How did she get away?" he asked.

"She just had a friend staying over with her Rottweiler, and he alerted them. When the friend went to check out what was going on, he saw a shape running, then heard the car start and speed off."

Dan drove until he hit the interstate, then stopped at the first truck stop. Walking in, he looked around before he slid into a booth and ordered coffee. How did he miss the roommate? He must have done something or said something that she saw and made her change her mind. He must stay on the path. The list won't let him go wrong, but he needed to kill. The urge was so strong that he could taste it. Looking around, he noticed a man staring at him. Smiling, he nodded his head in acknowledgment and continued with his coffee. Seeing movement, he noticed the guy slide closer to him. Looking at him closely, he could see the dirt and the wear on the man. Nodding his head, he looked away and grinned to himself. This would be so easy. Checking around, he nodded the guy over and watched as he picked up his coffee and walked to the booth. Sliding in, he said, "Hi, where ya heading, buddy?"

"North, but really anywhere is fine by me," he replied.

"Well, you can go my way. What is your name?"

"I'm Jason, and you?"

"Nice to meet ya, Jason. I'm Dan. I was planning on getting a room for the night. Stretch out and relax."

"Do you want to wait for me or would you want to share?"

"I wouldn't mind sharing with you if it's OK with you," Jason said.

"Sure, let's go. I saw a motel down the road; maybe they have a double bed open." Maybe the God's would smile down on him for this. Paying for the coffee, they headed outside. Pulling up outside the hotel, he kept looking around. Dark parking lot, and just to make sure he stayed out of the view of the hotel clerk. He sent Jason in to register while Dan compiled his checklist. Walking out with the key, he waved him toward the rooms and was glad when they went around back. He drove carefully behind him while he walked to the door, making sure no one was in the lot. Once it was open, Jason leaned against the door while he got out. Walking up, Jason grabbed him and kissed him against the door. Sliding the knife into his heart, Jason made a sound, and then all was quiet. Closing the door, he whistled while he worked. An hour later, when he left, he closed the door and drove away. Feeling better, he was much clearer on what he needed to do. All those stuck-up women who thought they were better than him had to die. And he was the one to do it. God was the smitter, and he was the hammer. Starting tomorrow, he would kill any woman that God spoke to him about.

"Matt's phone woke him up, and his captain said, Relief is there; we need you to come to the parking lot of the prescient right now." Driving up, he saw the police tape. "What's going on?" he asked as he got out.

"Our guy dropped us a present, literally," Christina said.

"Who is this?" he asked.

"We don't know, but it's our guy," said Christina as she walked up. He dropped her off, and no one saw anything.

"Did the cameras catch anything," he asked.

"We have staff going over that right now," she said.

The following morning, Jim showed up, and Matt invited him in.

"You might as well have breakfast while you wait. I could eat," he said. "Eggs and bacon coffee are on."

"Did they send you to check on me?" he asked as they headed back to the kitchen.

"Nope, I figured a good partner would come and grab food with his friend and check in."

Laughing, he replied, "You always were a smartass." While he poured the coffee, Jim slid on the stool and started talking. "The way I see it," he said, "this guy seems to think you are at fault and that you should have stopped him before he started. So, what did you do to piss off a psycho so badly that they killed over 160 women and still kept going?"

"Nothing, man. I have gone over and over, but this is a strange one."

"So, have you sat down and looked through your list? Yeah, but that seems to be a long shot. I mean, hell, I have been a cop for 10 years. Do you know how many people I come into contact with?"

"What about old cases? Have you written down who would want to get even?"

"Yeah, that is even more names."

"Well, it looks like it's going to be a long day. Let's get going, and we can divide it up and see where we end up."

At the end of the day, he found himself at a bar. Looking around as he picked up his drink, the door opened, and in walked Christina.

"I figured I would find you here," she said as she sat down.

"Help yourself to a seat," he replied as he took a long sip. "You know this isn't the way to figure this out. It seems to be working pretty well right now," he replied.

"That's it, let's go," she said.

"Where?"

"My house, I'm going to cook you a hot meal, and we can discuss this. You will feel better."

"I'm working pretty well on feeling better," he said as she took his beer.

"Hey, I was drinking that."

"Now you're following me to my house, and I'm going to cook. Don't make me say it again," she said as she started out. Walking to her door, he felt awkward. "It's only food," she said. As they sat around the kitchen counter and talked, he realized he did feel better. She kept him laughing with stories of her career, and he began to stop worrying. Looking at the clock, he said, "It's already 8 p.m., and I have to be in early. Thank you for the dinner, but I should be going."

"I have a spare bed," she said. "You really shouldn't drink and drive."

"You sure?" he said. Slowly, she put down her wine and said, "I hope you don't get offended by this," and kissed him. She felt him stiffen and went to pull away before his arms came around her, pulling her close. Fumbling with her buttons, he muttered against her mouth, "Bed?"

She said, "No time now. I need you now." Ripping his shirt open, she started kissing her way down his body at the top of his pants. She looked up and licked him above the buckle. Smiling, he wrapped his hand in her hair and pushed her down. As the pants fell to the ground, she took him in her mouth, and he groaned. "Oh god," he said. A few minutes later, he stopped her. "I don't want it to be over yet. My turn."

Laying her on the kitchen floor, he kneeled between her legs and nibbled his way up one leg to the thighs, then started over on the other leg. By the time he got to her thighs again, she was squirming. "Please," she said. With a wink, he leaned down and flicked his tongue over her once, then slowly exhaled his breath over her. Wrapping her hands in his hair, she jerked his head downward. "Enough, please," and then he dove down and slowly started licking, nibbling, and fingering her. Each time she would get close, he would back off until she was gushing. As she crested and laid there panting, he slid into her, making her gasp. Building speed, she was scratching his back and biting his neck to keep from screaming. He kept hitting her spot until she couldn't take it. As her eyes rolled in the back of her head, he pulled out and shot everything he had on her belly. Dropping down beside her, he laughed.

"You were right; this is what I needed."

"Glad to help," she replied.

Across town, Officer Martin looked up as the doctor walked toward him.

"Evening," he said as he went to step in.

"Hold on, Doc, I have to see your badge," he said.

"Sure." Holding it up, Dan waited.

"Go ahead in," he said.

As he walked softly to the bed. He kept muttering to himself, *I can't believe you survived*, he said. "It's a shame really you have to die like this, all peaceful instead of screaming." Holding up a syringe, he put it in her IV line and turned, walking out. A few minutes later, Officer Martin heard code blue and saw everyone running toward him.

"What happened?" he asked.

"Move," said a nurse. Pushing past him, he saw Sarah wasn't breathing, and the machines had flat lines. Picking up his phone, he called Captain.

"There's a problem; you need to get here now. Sarah Jennings is dead."

When his phone rang, Matt knew something bad had happened. Picking it up, he said, "Yeah, listening."

He sat up and said, "Don't worry, I'm on my way. I'll tell her she is right here."

"Yeah, we were having dinner discussing the case. Hanging up." He just dropped his head.

"What happened, Matt?"

"Sarah is dead."

"How?"

"Some man dressed as a doctor went in, and after he left, she was dead."

"While I was here with you, she died."

"Matt, it's not your fault; this fucker would have gotten her even if you had been there."

"Maybe, but she died while I was getting off. I have to go," he said.

"Give me a minute; I'll be ready, and we can go together."

An hour later, he pulled into his space at the prescient and just laid his head on the wheel. He couldn't believe she was dead. If only he had been at the hospital.

Sighing, he got out of his car and started inside when a man walked up and said, "Officer Cartwright?"

"Yes, that's me."

"This is for you," he said, handing him an envelope and running away.

"Hey, wait, you hey you," he yelled, but the man kept running.

Turning, he walked into the building and put the envelope on the scanner to see what it was.

"Looks like pictures to me," said the guard.

"Yeah, Harvey, it's pictures, but pictures of what?" he asked.

"I don't know, and you won't either, unless you open it," he says, laughing.

"I think I need to do this upstairs."

At his desk, he dropped into his chair and opened the envelope, and pictures of Sarah Jennings came tumbling out. "Oh Jesus," he yelled as he dropped the envelope, causing everyone to look up.

His boss walked over, said, "What's," then saw the pictures.

"I think this needs to be taken to the room." He gathered up everything, and everyone walked in behind him.

"Matt, how did you get these pictures?"

"A guy approached me in the parking lot, asked for me by name, and handed them to me."

"Can you describe him?"

"Yeah, Captain, I can." As the police artist sat with him, he kept going over the description.

"Is this him?" he asked, holding up a piece of paper. "Yeah," he said. "That's the guy."

"OK, I'll start a run on him and hopefully get something. The ME said he needed to talk to you when you were done here." Heading out, he saw Christina look up as he went to the elevator. Pushing the button for the morgue, he waited, and getting off, he saw the ME at his desk.

"Hey, Gus, you wanted to see me?"

"Yeah, the bastard didn't clean this one. We got DNA. I just put it in CODIS, but it will take a day or so to get it back. You should go home and sleep. I have patients that look better than you do right now."

Pamela Houston walked up to speak to Matt.

"How's it going?" she asked.

"It's fine, Pam. What do you want?"

"My lawyer said you haven't signed the divorce papers yet."

"Why not? Pam, I told you I wanted my attorney to go over them. You are asking for a lot."

Laughing, she said, "You have no idea."

"Look, pam, what we had was a mistake, and I am not going to hash this out again. I will sign them when my attorney is finished and we make a revision. Until then, we have nothing to talk about. Now, if you will excuse me, I have to get back to work."

Watching him, she said, "What you think you caused this?"

Looking up, he said, "What do you know? Nothing; I just heard the guy was out to get you." Laughing, she walked away. "It's nice to know that I'm not the only one who hates your guts."

Dan sat at the bar, looking around as he sipped his beer. He was playing a game.

"What did each loser do for a living?" With humor in his eyes, he called the waitress over. "Getcha?" she asked. "Another bud and some chili fries." Handing him the beer, her attention shifted to the TV. Turning it up, she heard as the death toll rises in these grisly murders, police are declining to respond. Four women in two weeks all brutally murdered. What are the police doing to protect us? We will keep you updated as the story develops. Shaking her head, she turned back to him.

"Can you believe this?" she said.

"In society today, you can't predict what a person is thinking or doing."

"Ain't that the truth?" Sliding his fries at him, she winked and turned away. As he ate, he watched her work. Smiling and laughing, she was very pretty. Seeing he was finished, she walked down another bud.

"No two is my limit," he responded. Pulling forty dollars out of his wallet, he handed it to her and said, "Keep the change."

"Wow, thanks!" she said, smiling.

"Listen, would you be interested in having dinner with me sometime?"

"That's sweet," she replied, "but I don't date patrons, and I'm already dating someone."

"No big deal," he said gruffly. Heading to his car, he kept replaying the night. How dare she flirt with him, leading him on to turn him down? He could just picture her laughing and joking about him. By the time he got home, he had a different look for the night. He could see her touching him and flirting with him, and when he asked her out, she laughed like a looser, like, you? No thank you, jerk, before walking away. *I'll teach her*, he said. Slamming his door, she's nothing but a whore. What right did she have to treat me like that and then keep all my money? Looking up, Matt heard his captain yelling. He caught up to him at the elevator. Bastard left one alive hospital now! Sliding into the car, he held on as they raced off. Running into the hospital, he saw FBI agents and local cops everywhere. As everyone began talking at once, Christina raised her voice.

"Stop everyone, just stop. Now we know that at 3:15 a.m. Mike Johnson came out of his bar to lock up and noticed a bartender's car still in the parking lot. As he approached, he called her name and saw a man jerk up and run off. Miss Kimberly Prickles is our victim. She had gotten off work at 3 a.m. There were a lot of male clients in tonight, but Mike thinks he can describe a few. Other than being knocked out, Miss Prickles is fine. The hospital is keeping her overnight for observation. Matt, we want you with her for the first shift. Got it covered and walked away." Going to the room, he noticed the doctor was in with her.

"Excuse me, doctor?"

"Hello, I was just checking on the patient."

"May I get your name?"

"Sure, Doctor Dan H. Yearly."

Pulling out a pager, he said, "Please excuse me, I'm being paged." Walking out, he closed the door, and Matt sat. Picking up a pen, he started writing names. Hearing the door open, he saw a doctor walk in.

"May I help you," he said.

"Yes, I'm Dr. Craig Lewis, and I'm here to see how my patient is doing."

"Where is the doctor yearly?"

"I'm sorry I don't know a doctor yearly."

"He was just in here."

"Sir, I assure you, there is no doctor Yearly on call tonight, nor on staff, to my knowledge." Yanking out his phone, he barked, "Christina, get me the security guard and the footage. I think he was just here."

"Let me make a call; your replacement will meet you, and I'll be waiting at the front office." Looking through the footage, he yelled, "Stop there, that's the guy. Where do I know him from? Let's get this to the station and get the guys on it."

Christina said, "In the meantime, I want you to stay with our bartender until we get her witness protection. Maybe she can tell us about this guy."

Waking up, she turned her head and saw a cop sitting and looking at a piece of paper. She must have made a sound because he was there in a second.

"It's OK, I'm Matt Cartwright with the police department. You're in the hospital, safe. I'm here, and we are going to keep you safe." Licking her lips, she motioned for water, which he brought to her lips. "Do you remember what happened?"

"I remember I got off at 3 a.m. And I was thinking about how much I hate working the night shift, but I need the money, and weekends are my best nights. As I approached my car, I noticed the flat tire. Great, just what I need. Looking around, the parking lot was empty and black. I whirled when I heard a noise, but nothing was there. What was the noise?" Matt asked.

"It sounded like a footstep, but when I went to turn back around, I didn't know anything after that other than waking up here." As she replayed what happened, he asked, "Do you know the guy that asked you out?"

"Not really. He said his name was Dan. Other than that, he came in several times a week and always sat at the same spot. If it was occupied, he would wait until they left to sit down."

"Do you think you can describe him to a police artist?" he asked.

"Yeah, I can; he was really nice and a good tipper. Tonight, he tipped me almost 15 dollars."

"Do you still have the money?"

"It should be in my purse," she replied.

"We will get fingerprints and start a run on them," he said as an officer walked in.

"Officer Lendoff, how are you?"

"I'm good, sir. I'm here to sit with Miss Prickles while you go to the office."

Walking in, he saw everyone was in the meeting room. As he stepped in, Christina asked if he had the list.

"Yeah here it is. All three pages. Let's get the names ran though NCIC and see what pops." Sitting in the meeting room, Matt and Jim went through everything.

"Man, I didn't know you knew all these people. Let's look at people with medical backgrounds since the cuts are so precise, then pull the ones that live out of state and put them in one pile, then divide them into professions." 30 minutes later, they had five piles.

"OK, we have four doctors, two dentists, and a handful of nurses." Picking up the first file, he looked. "Hey, I remember Benny. He was the chubby kid that used to tag along with me and a couple of guys. He was always really slow, though. I don't see him doing this." Putting it down, he went through two more before he picked up a file. "Man, I forgot about Dan Andrews. He really became a doctor."

"Why does that surprise you," said Jim.

"Well, he was always morbid and dark. Laughed at movies where people died, wanting to reenact the scene. I heard from a kid that he was killing animals and…" He looked up. "I had forgotten he used to skin the animals." A sharp knock at the door had everyone looking up. The prints come back to Doctor Dan Andrews. "That's Dan's name, but that isn't the man I saw tonight, unless he is very good at disguising himself. Let's get a bolo out for him and have a talk."

Chapter Five

Dan and Jane sat watching the news when a picture of him popped up. Turning it up, he listened.

"Damn time to move," he said. Looking at Jane, he wished she would stop her yammering; all she had ever done was nag at him and bitched.

Sighing, he went to start packing; it wouldn't be long before the cops tracked him down. Looking around, he thought he had gotten everything. Walking to the living room, he looked at Jane and realized he would miss her as he walked out the door.

The address on file for Dan and Jane Andrews is a couple blocks from here. "Full-gear guys, we don't know what we are walking into." Pulling up, he could hear Jim bitching about the gear.

"It's heavy and itchy."

"Yeah, but at least you get to go home tonight," he heard someone say.

"Lights are on, no movement he heard through the earpiece." Getting out, they ducked down. 10 minutes later, still no movement before his captain said, "Let's move in slowly." As they eased up the walkway, they kept alert but couldn't hear anything. Yelling police, they kicked in the door, and everyone started gagging. Covering their noses and mouths, they walked in, and there on the couch were two skeletons. Fully peeled and propped up like they were watching the TV that was on. "Who the hell is this?" Christina asked.

"I don't know. Let's clear the house, get the ME in here, and get dental started. I think we just found Jane Andrews, but who is the male?"

Several blocks over, he sat watching the police laughing. *Pussies*, he said to himself. He sure was going to miss hearing Jane's voice, but he could always replay what he had.

A couple days later, the ME walked in with the file. "Your skeletons were Jane Andrews and Dan Andrews. They have been dead for approximately three weeks. If he was dead, then how was he in the hospital, the bar, and at work?"

"I think the guy was wearing his skin," replied the ME.

"At the airport, Dan walked into the women's room and into a stall, taking off the skin. He was sad. I really will miss this," he said, "but at least I have more." Unzipping his bag, he pulled out a plastic bag and slid it open. Sliding the skin into the bag, she walked out.

"Hello, Pamela," she said, looking in the mirror with a smile. Walking out of the restroom, she went to the counter and got a ticket.

As she boarded the plane, Matt and Jim were starting to look through the list again.

"Why were you willing to dismiss that one guy, Benny?"

"Yeah, Benny Goode, he was a slow kid looking back. I think he was almost mentally retarded, but in my day, we didn't say things like that. He was always a happy kid, and he followed a group of us around like a puppy."

"But he was smart enough to become a dentist," replied Jim.

"What has he been up to these past few years?"

"Well, looking at his file, he was married with kids. The wife left him about five years ago, and, hmmm that's strange."

"What?" said Matt.

"He hasn't filed a tax return in the past five years."

"OK, so he isn't paying the IRS a big deal."

"No, I mean, he hasn't filed, he hasn't used his bank account credit card, nothing. It looks like five years ago, Benny Goode walked off the face of the earth. The last activity on his account, he withdrew, whistling," he said. "Almost two million dollars."

"That type of money could go anywhere," Matt said.

"Yeah, but there is no plane ticket, no house, and nothing in his name. Let's get started looking for Benny Goode now," said Matt, jumping up. "Can we get a sketch of what he would look like now?"

"Sure," replied Jim, "but I don't think it will do us any good." Walking out to the elevator, Matt suddenly stopped. "Hey captain, has anyone put out a bolo for this Dan guy since we know he is wearing Dan's face? Maybe we can get him that way." Heading out to his car, he figured he would swing by a couple hotels and maybe someone would recognize him. After several hours, he was getting angry. No one had seen the man, and no one had booked in or out with his name. How did he live? Getting an idea, he pulled over and called Christina.

"Hey, can you find local realtors and see about houses that have been rented out? This guy has to either have a house or he has a partner, and I really hope that it's the first one. Having two of these wacko's would not be good."

The next morning, as Matt sat at his desk looking over the rental list, he couldn't believe how many they were. "Let's focus on short-term rentals, and male occupants," said Christina, "then go from there."

On Friday, Matt and Jim sat at the office.

"It's been a week, Jim. No activity, nothing. Who was this guy?" A call just came in saying there has been an explosion on County Road 85 at the old turner place. The realtor just called. It was rented out two months ago to Tom Andrews. Picking up their jackets, they headed out. Pulling up, they sat wow. Any evidence is long gone. As before, they sat in a hole the size of the town. They got out an FBI agent with the tag BOMB SQUAD met them. "From what we can see, there were at least five sticks of C4 used here. He leveled the place and everything within 2000 feet of it. There is a garage standing half a mile away, but I'm not sure if it belongs to this house or not."

"We will look just to be sure," said Matt.

Walking over, they all stood while the K9 dog sniffed. "I'm sorry guys, it's wired," the agent said. "We can't let you go in until we know what to do, and that will take time." As he finished his sentence, the ground started to rumble. "Run!" he shouted as the first explosion hit the air. Ducking behind the vehicle, they watched as the garage exploded into the air in a ball of flames. Standing, they couldn't believe it until pictures started falling out of the sky. Different women different poses, all in different stages of torture and death. Picking up a photo, he said, "Well, let's find out who Tom Andrews is, was, or if he even existed."

On Monday, they were no closer to the truth when he saw his captain talking with an ups guy. "What's up, captain?" he asked.

"There was a package left at the airport that was shipped to Chicago and back with your name on it. It's Dan Andrews's skin, and there is a card for you."

"What did it say?"

"The card said this is farewell, but not the end. I will speak to you soon. This time, there was a mouth."

Matt looked up as Christina walked toward him. "There have been no more deaths here in two weeks, so our office has called us back. We are going to file this with the others, and if we get any more leads, we will let you know."

On Wednesday, Gus came tearing into the squad room. "Matt, look, I ran that sample through the database, and it came back female. Matt, we aren't looking for a man; we are looking for a woman. I turned the skin wrong side out, and I got fingerprints. I put them in the system and will hopefully get something."

"That's fine, Gus, the FBI is gone, so we are supposed to just file anything we get in a cold case and send it to them to be put on the shelf."

Matt said his captain looking out.

"You need to come in here."

"What's up," he said, noticing that Christina was in the office.

"Hey, I thought you guys had closed these and left. We did until Gus called us and told us the fingerprints came back. You might want to sit down for this."

"Who did they belong to?"

"Matt, its Pam. Pam, as in my soon-to-be ex-wife? I know the woman is crazy, but you have got the wrong person."

"Pamela isn't that crazy."

"Matt, we triple-checked them; it's her," Christina said. "Do you know where she is?"

"I'll call her right now and have her come in. You are way off base." Walking to his captain's desk, he picked up the phone and dialed a number. Waiting, he heard the machine and went to speak, then stopped.

"Matt, if this is you, I guess you found my prints. I can't tell you how much fun I had and your face each time. I warned you when you left me that you would regret it. Remember, this is your fault. Goodbye," and laughing it ended. Dropping the phone, he sat down.

"Pamela couldn't do this," he said.

"Matt, look at me." Christina bent down; we have to find her. We looked into her background, and before five years ago, "Pamela Houston never existed."

"Five years?" you said.

"Yeah why?"

"Jim walked in five years ago; Benny Goode disappeared, and no one has seen or heard from him. I just got off the phone with a doctor in New Jersey, and he said someone matching that description came in, paid a lot of money, and walked out a woman. It's been so long that they have to look for the file, but I bet that Benny is Pamela."

As Matt sat at his desk, Pamela sat in London, smiling and laughing. She toasted herself for a job well done. "Let's see if he can follow my clues," she said to the room. As he sat looking over the file, his phone rang.

"Hey Matt, it's Christina, are you busy?"

"No, I got time to talk."

"I'm in Newborn, Ohio, and there is a dead male. I think it's our girl."

"Why do you think that?"

"She left your card at the scene. We have been tracking her since she left Texas. We have a body in Arkansas, Oklahoma, Chicago, and now Ohio. We were hoping to leave you out of this, but the higher-ups want us to bring you to Washington until further notice. Your boss has already cleared you, and your bags are packed. Wheels up in 30."

"I'll see you soon," he said, hanging up.

The following morning, as he sat in the room, he looked around at all the FBI agents and thought about how a couple months could make a difference. He stared at the board and wondered how he couldn't have seen that Pamela, wait, no Benny was capable of doing something like this. He still couldn't believe that Pamela was really Benny. His attorney had gone to court, and they had vacated the marriage, at least, so as far as the court was concerned, he had never been married. Feeling a vibration, he picked up his cell phone and saw a blocked call. Putting it on speaker, he said, "Cartwright."

"Matt, how are you holding up?"

"Hello Benny."

"Now, now Matt, my name is Pamela. It says so on the birth certificate you saw."

"Where are you, Pamela? We can chat face-to-face? Soon, but not yet, first you have to find me. Are we having fun, Matt?" she said, laughing.

"Fun, Pamela! you killed over 175 people. I think it's time to sit and talk. What did they do to you?" Making a motion, the FBI agent leaned forward.

"Sorry, Matt. As much as I would love to sit and talk, I have to cut this short. I'll be in touch, but I hope you enjoy your next gift from me. It was the most exhilarating feeling ever!"

Picking up the files, he storms angrily to the door.

"Matt, hold on, we can catch her. You have the brains of all of us; you're not working this alone anymore. How are we going to catch her," he said? Walking out the door, he got to the rental car when he felt something hit him in the shoulder before he went down. When he came, he was in the hospital bed, and Christina was standing and looking at him. "Another inch to the left, and you would be dead."

"What the hell happened?" he asked.

"Someone shot you, but it wasn't with a bullet; it was with a bone. They pulled it out, and we got it to DNA. Oh God, Matt, when I came out after you and saw you on the ground, it scared me. Do we have any leads?"

"Not yet, but we have all our officers working on the cameras; we have to get something." As the doctor walked in, Matt stared at him for a second before saying, "Doc, can I see some ID? Nothing personal, but after everything."

Laughing, Christina said, "Matt, meet my father, Marcus Crystals. He is the best surgeon in DC and maybe the whole east coast."

"Son, you were lucky. I'm sure Christina already told you. We are going to release you into her custody, but you should rest. If you have any fever, pain, or substance oozing out of the wound, you need to come back here ASAP."

The next morning over coffee, they talked, and Christina said, "You were so tired last night we didn't want to wake you, but they got a hit. The DNA came back to Mike Chaffer; he was a homeless man who had been in and out of jail for intoxication charges. We sent a notification to his next of kin. He went off the radar of the local police about a month ago. They had hoped he had gotten help. Son of a bitch," he said. "Why is she doing this?"

"Matt, you and I both know that you can't predict if a person is sane or not. The best thing we can do is track her down and stop her. And the only way to do that is to start at the beginning. Tell me about when you two met."

"It was Valentine's Day a year ago. I was eating dinner when she bumped into me, spilling her wine down my shirt. She was so flustered, I offered her a seat, and we started talking. It seemed like we had so much in common that the restaurant that we were at actually ended up asking us to leave so they could close. We walked out to a bench and talked all night. When the sun came up, I asked her to my house, and she never left. Two months later, we were married, and it was only after that that I realized that she wasn't who she had pretended to be."

"How so?"

"Well, she told me her parents had died in a gas accident, but she started slipping, and I found out that her dad had killed her mom and then himself. I let it slide because I figured she was ashamed to say anything, but then money started missing and she had a short fuse. You know, one time I was late to dinner. By 5 minutes, I came home, and she had destroyed all my clothes, broken every dish I had, and sliced her wrist. I called 911, and when the EMT's got there, she tried to tell them that I did it. That night, I filed for a restraining order and divorce papers and refused to speak to her."

"The past couple of months, she had been showing up at my job to ask for a second chance, but I refused to speak to her. The judge had her put in jail for 10 days for violating the restraining order, but she acted like I chose to leave and that I didn't love her and that I was cheating on her. Any woman who said hello to me was accused of sleeping with me."

"That might be what set her off. As of now, anything you can remember about her parents' names or any family members that might help us is vital."

"I can do that;" he said. "She was an only child with no close family that I could recall, but knowing it's Benny, we have to start over and run a new history. I know it's hard, but we must continue calling her Pamela so she doesn't become more enraged than she already is."

Chapter Six

Walking into the FBI headquarters the next morning, he stopped short.

"Sarah, is that you?"

"Oh, Matt, you weren't supposed to see me. We felt it was best if I died so she would forget about me. She almost killed me that day." Turning around, he started yelling at Christina, "How dare you? I thought she was dead. I grieved for her. Who did we bury? No one, it was an empty casket and no one will ever know that she didn't die. I think it's time we caught you up to date."

"Sarah started receiving these calls, and we were able to trace one to Driscoll, which is why we had her go there. We never imagined anyone else would get hurt. But when we moved her, the killings intensified, and then they paused when they started back up in Driscoll, which shocked us all. That is why we came. We had to do damage control. We never expected her to be attacked in our custody, and after the bosses heard, they wanted us to take her out of play, so when the killer went to the hospital, we saw it as our chance to move her quietly. She has been here in DC, running names and like crimes, and working behind the scenes."

"I can't believe you didn't trust me enough to tell me," he said as he turned away. Reaching out to touch him, she dropped her hand and turned.

"So, what have you found?"

"Well, after Benny became Pamela, she went on a shopping spree. She loves high-end products and flew over seas a couple times to get some."

"Do we know where she flew to?" ask Christina. "Yeah, she flew to London a couple times and to France. She always talked about France," Matt said. "She always said that once I retired, she wanted us to move to a little town there."

"What town?"

"Hmm, let me think a second. It was Dijon. I remember because I laughed and told her I wasn't moving to a town named after a mustard. She got mad that night and slept on the couch."

"Good, Matt, keep thinking anything else?"

"She always said she would see the world. Start at the Berlin Wall and then go until she had to stop, and wherever she was, she would live. She talked about Cockatoo Island a lot and then shut up when she realized I thought she was joking."

Jumping up, Sarah said, "Alright, people, let's get in touch with INTERPOL and get her picture faxed over. I want some answers. Did she fly out anywhere? Start looking at the flight manifest for single women leaving the country. Run background on every one of them. It's go time, people," she said. "And the clock is running."

Chapter Seven

When they got off work that evening, he asked for a recommendation for a hotel. "Matt, come on, you don't have to do that," she said. "My guest room is still open. Christina, you let me think she was dead. I felt guilty; it almost destroyed me. And to find out she was alive here the whole time. You should have told me. I need to get a room and be alone tonight," he said. Fine pulling up, she dropped him outside a local hotel.

"This is a good hotel," she said. "Tell them you're working with my team, and they will take care of you," she said as she pulled off. Walking in, he got a room and went and just sat on the edge of the bed. The events of the day catching up to him, so he laid down in his clothes and dozed off. He woke to a pounding on the door. Looking through the peephole, he opened it up.

"What's wrong?" he asked.

"Matt, you have to come to the office. We found Pamela, but she is dead."

"What do you mean dead," he asked?

"She was found today in London at a hotel dead. The ME is doing a run, but room service had been ordered for two, Matt. We don't think she was working alone."

"I'll be ready in five," he said as he walked to the bed. "Matt," Christina said looking up, he saw her hesitate. "There was a note, and on it the words 'Copycat.' I don't know what to make of it, do you?"

"Give me a minute, would you?"

Walking out, she closed the door, and he picked up the phone. "Jim, it's me; they found Pamela killed, and a note that said copycat on it. Really said, Jim, that it sounds like she made someone mad at me."

"Yeah, I know I need you here with me. Can you come?"

"Sure thing."

"Be on the first flight out."

Hanging up, he just sat. He couldn't believe the woman he was married to was dead. Even after all that had happened, it had made him sad.

Melissa sat at the coffee shop waiting to meet her pen pal. She was both scared and excited out of everything impulsive she had done, and agreeing to meet her at this time was crazy. Sipping her coffee, she noticed her watch and looked at her phone. Her friend was 30 minutes late, and as she went to message her, a text popped up from an unknown number. As she read it, she knocked over her coffee. The text said, *You can consider yourself lucky; this is your one free pass. Don't do anything stupid like this again.* Picking up her phone, she called the police and sat down to wait. While she waited, it seemed everyone was watching her and monitoring her. Every little movement and sound had her jerking. By the time the police got to the coffee shop, she was shaking. When they had taken her statement, she asked if they would follow her home and make sure she got in safely. Driving home, she thought she saw someone following her. As they pulled up behind her, she asked them to walk her in and check her house. One of the officers assured her that everything was OK. Locking her door, she thought for a moment, then decided she had to leave. Picking up a suitcase, she started throwing things in and didn't stop when some fell to the floor. The phone beeping had her stopping, and with dread, she read the text. *You don't have to leave; I will always be watching over you. Call this number and ask for Matt Cartwright. He will tell you I keep my word. Enjoy your life; just remember, I will only be a whisper away.* Dropping her phone, she ran out the door and drove straight to the police station. As she waited for Matt Cartwright to come down, she sat praying for help. Walking into the building, Matt wondered what had set the killer off. Introducing himself, he had to stop her several times to calm down. Finally, when she was out of breath, he said, "Miss Christopher, I am just here helping the FBI with a case. I'm not sure how your case connects to mine, but I will see what the FBI wants to do. For tonight, why don't you let me get you a hotel room at our cost?" He inserted when she started protesting. "Then tomorrow morning, we will come over and get a file started with us. This will give us time to talk to the local police and get their report." Walking to the elevator, he called Christina and asked her to meet him. Sitting at an empty desk, they went over all the woman had said.

"Why lure her there and scare her, and why send her to you?" Christina asked.

"Let's get her phone logs and computer and start looking."

"Matt, it's almost midnight; there isn't much we can do. Why don't you go to bed and we can start fresh in the morning?"

As he lay in bed, the case kept going around in his head. He suddenly sat up and dialed Christina.

"Pick up Pick up," he muttered. "Hey, I have an idea. Meet me at Miss Christopher's house." Pulling up, she got out of the car and found him with coffee for her.

"Light and sweet, just the way you like it," he said.

"I just might forgive you for waking me up. So, what is this idea?"

"I know how he is stalking her."

"Her who?"

"The lady Miss Christopher. Her bank records show that she recently updated her home security so she could go automated with everything, the TV, the lights, the door locks, everything."

"OK, and that means what?"

"Follow me on this: when you have a handyman in your home, do you stand over his shoulder or do you let him do his work and come check in?"

"I show him what needs to be done, and then I leave him to it."

"Exactly I am willing to bet that if we check, some of our victims had a handyman of some kind in their house in the previous months."

"How are you so sure?"

"Let me show you." Walking through the house, he stopped. "Does something look wrong with this room?"

"Yeah, that chair is at an odd angle; it's facing away from the rest of the furniture." Picking it up, he found a tiny camera on it. Holding it up, he said, "See, I told you. I'm willing to bet that there are more of these throughout the house. He does it under their noses to prove that he is smarter than they are. The rush of possibly getting caught keeps him going." Looking at the camera, he says, "I will find you, and I won't stop until I do. I promise you on all that I hold, I will find you and make you pay for what you have done." Throwing the camera down, he walked out into the night… To be continued.